This is for Richard – J.S.

Text copyright © Jeremy Strong 1999
Illustrations copyright © David Mostyn 1999

First published in Great Britain in 1999
by Macdonald Young Books
an imprint of Wayland Publishers Ltd
61 Western Road
Hove
East Sussex
BN3 1JD

Find Macdonald Young Books on the internet at
http://www.myb.co.uk

Designed and Typeset by Backup Creative Services, Dorset DT10 1DB
Printed in Hong Kong

British Library Cataloguing in Publication Data available

ISBN: 0 7500 2680 4

JEREMY STRONG

Max and the Haunted Castle

Illustrated by David Mostyn

MACDONALD YOUNG BOOKS

Chapter One

Max's dad had been inventing in his little shed all night, and now he looked madder than ever. His hair stuck out from his head like some enormous wild plant. His eyes boggled behind his thick spectacles. He grinned across the breakfast table at Max.

"I've done it!"

Max swallowed a spoonful of Spooky Chunks. (*Spooky Chunks! The crunchy wheat cereal that comes in the shapes of ghosties and ghoulies!*) "What have you done?" he asked politely.

"Allow me to demonstrate," said Max's dad grandly. He put his hands to his spectacles. The lenses began to twirl and whirl, giving off dizzying flashes of bright light.

Max was transfixed, with a spoonful of Spooky Chunks frozen half-way to his mouth. He could not move. He could not speak. A strange, helpless noise dribbled from his open mouth, "Durrrrrr...?"

"Are you sure this is safe?" asked Max's mum.

"Of course it is. Just you watch. Max has been thoroughly hypnotized by my amazing Hypno-spex. I'm going to give Max some orders now and he will have to obey them. Max, go and feed the cat."

Max marched stiffly towards Ginger, who was sitting quietly on the window sill.

He was lazily dreaming about catching that noisy starling out in the garden when all at once Max tried to feed him with a large spoonful of Spooky Chunks.

"*Yeiouaw!*"

Ginger leaped on to Max's head and then took a flying dive that sent him sprawling across the kitchen table. Breakfast was instantly scattered in several different directions at once, mostly downwards. Plates and bowls smashed on the tiles. Pools of milk and cereal and soggy toast slopped across the floor.

"I thought you said it was safe," sighed Max's mum.

Max's dad looked disappointed. "That wasn't meant to happen. Max wasn't supposed to feed Ginger with Spooky Chunks."

"Well I have just invented something of my own," snapped Max's mum.

"Really? What's that, delight of my life?"

"It's a new kitchen cleaner and it clears messes just like this. It does everything: washing, drying, polishing, cleaning, even putting away."

"That's brilliant!" Max's dad was very impressed.

"Yes," Mum went on. "It's called *you*! You can clear this kitchen, but before you do I suggest you unhypnotize Max. It's time he went to school."

Max's dad pulled off his Hypno-spex, revealing another pair of boggly spectacles underneath. As he tidied the kitchen he told Max about his latest invention. Max was quite impressed, although he wasn't sure what anyone would want a pair of Hypno-spex for.

Max grabbed his bag and set off for school, leaving his dad cleaning the kitchen and his mum upstairs, where she was skiing. (Max's mum had a ski-exercising machine.)

Since it was a bit boring skiing in the bedroom she had a poster of Mount Everest pinned on the wall so that she could imagine she was skiing down it. Sometimes she deliberately crashed and fell over (just to make things more realistic.)

Chapter Two

When Max reached school he got a surprise. In fact the whole class got a surprise, and it was a rather nice one, too.

"On Friday our class will be going on an outing," announced Miss Blossom. "As you know, we have been studying 'Invaders' this term at school. We are going to visit a Norman castle. The youngest children will be coming with us. You can help look after them."

This last announcement caused a few groans. However, everyone was very excited about visiting a castle. Everyone except Gripper Grabbly, leader of the Grabbly Gang. There were three of them, all brothers, and Gripper was the oldest. He had a big head and big ears and a big, noisy mouth. "Out of my way, you horrible earwig!" he would shout, "or I'll squeeze you to bits!"

Of course, if you were very brave (and stupid) you could try saying: "Buzz off Gripper! You've got a face like a rhino's bottom! Go away and leave me alone." Funnily enough, nobody *ever* said things like that to Gripper Grabbly. Snitch was the middle brother. He had sneaky weasel eyes and big teeth that stuck out. Snitch spent most of the time grinning and saying "Yeah!" every time Gripper threatened to bash someone (which was quite often).

The smallest Grabbly was called Squad Car, because he was always pretending to be a police car. He went rushing round the playground going 'dee-doo, dee-doo, dee-doo!' very loudly.

Gripper Grabbly was not at all impressed by the news of the outing. "Boring old castle," he growled. "Who wants to see a boring old castle?"

"I do," said Max, who was looking forward to it.

Gripper Grabbly leaned across his table and sneered at Max. "Yeah, well you would, wouldn't you, Frog-eyes." And he laughed noisily, because he thought he was being very funny.

Out in the playground Gripper Grabbly soon found his two brothers. He marched them to a quiet corner and they huddled together, whispering.

"We don't want to go to some stupid old castle," grumbled Gripper. Snitch nodded, while Squad Car kept quiet. Actually he did want to see the castle, but he knew better than to argue with his big brothers. "Anyhow, I've got a plan. We're going to make this visit the most exciting visit ever."

"How will we do that?" asked Snitch, wrinkling his weasel nose.

"We're going to scare the pants off everyone!" smirked Gripper. Squad Car's eyes grew round with wonder.

"Scare their pants off! Even the teach...!" He began to giggle hysterically.

"Stupid! I don't mean *really* scare their pants off, I mean we'll give them a really nasty fright. We'll have them screaming and trembling – they're such a bunch of limpy-wimpy chickens. Now listen to me. This is what we do..."

Chapter Three

Breakfast time in Max's house seemed to be a bit of a disaster area. Max's dad was trying out yet another new invention. It was a little black box with a mini rotor blade sticking up from the top. A small metal scoop poked out from the front.

"This is brilliant!" cried Max's dad. "This is my Auto-feeder. It has a microchip that has been programmed to automatically dip the spoon into your cereal bowl and carry the food to your mouth. It leaves your hands free to do lots of other things."

"Like what?" asked Max.

"You could paint your bedroom or make paper hats or knit yourself a scarf... go on, please try it out for me."

So Max tried out the automatic spoon. It whizzed about like some mini UFO, feeding him with Spooky Chunks, while he sat there twiddling his thumbs. Then it went wrong and began to go faster and faster. Max couldn't keep up.

He was still chewing one spoonful of cereal when the next arrived, so the Auto-feeder tipped it down his face, and then another load arrived, and another.

"Stop-spplurrrgh!" choked Max.

Dad tried to switch off the spoon, but now it was grabbing cereal and tipping it everywhere – over Dad's spectacles, on Mum's head, in Ginger's ear! Spooky-Chunks were everywhere and still the spoon was zooming about.

One moment it was flicking sugar across the table and the next it was scooping up marmalade and bombing the coffee mugs. *Shlopp!* Tidal waves of coffee slopped across the table and dribbled on to the floor. At last Max's mum managed to stop the spoon by swatting it with a very large frying pan. *SPLANGG!* She glared at her husband. "Time I used my cleaning invention again," she said. "Go on. Get on with it."

"I'd better wash first," groaned Max's dad.

"Me too," said Max, and they went to the bathroom together.

"You'd better hurry up," his mum said. "It's your outing to the castle today."

Oh no! Why did everything go wrong just when Max had something important to do? He hastily rubbed his face dry, picked up his spectacles, raced downstairs, grabbed his packed lunch and ran like the wind to school.

He was almost at the school gates before he realized he was wearing the wrong spectacles, but it was too late to go back and change them. He had a school outing to go on, and he didn't want to miss that! He gazed blearily through his father's glasses. Oh well, he would just have to put up with them.

Chapter Four

The castle was brilliant. It had battlements and dungeons and a moat and huge oak doors. It was just what Max thought a castle ought to be like. He wandered round with his friends, getting more and more excited.

The Grabbly Gang were not impressed. "What a titchy castle," sneered Gripper. He snorted at the dungeon. "It's so cosy, I wouldn't mind living here."

Squad Car gave his big brother an anxious look. He didn't want to live in a dungeon at all. He stuck his thumb in his mouth and held tightly on to Snitch's hand.

At lunch-time the children gathered on the grass inside the castle walls and unloaded their bags. Packed lunches were the best part of any school trip.

"Follow me," whispered Gipper to his brothers, and slipped behind a wall. Squad Car had just taken a bite from his sandwich and was most upset to be dragged away.

"Stop snivelling!" hissed Gripper. "In a moment you can have as much food as you like. We're going to scare those nimby-pimbies right off their lunch!"

"What's a nimby-pimby?" asked Snitch, but Gripper just scowled at him.

"Stupid!" he said, as if everyone knew what a nimby-pimby was.

Gripper undid his bag and pulled out three white bedsheets. "Put these over your heads," he ordered his brothers. "We're going to be ghastly ghosts! Now, when I count to three, we rush out making ghostie noises and scare everyone for miles and then we eat all their lunches!"

"Brilliant!" giggled Snitch.

"What noises do ghosties make?" asked Squad Car.

"They go 'whooooooo' of course. OK? Right, ready... One, two, three, GO!"

Out rushed the Grabbly Ghosts, flapping their sheets and making dreadful, spine-chilling noises.

"Whooooooooo!" went the biggest ghost.

"Oooooo!" went the middle-sized ghost.

"Dee-doo, dee-doo!" went the smallest ghost.

"Aargh! Ghosts! Help! Save us!"

There was instant panic. Children screamed and scrambled for safety, climbing over each other in their haste to escape from the advancing ghouls. Lunch was abandoned as the children fled in all directions, while poor Miss Blossom did her best to gather them together and comfort them.

Gripper stopped on the grass and sniggered. "Scaredy-cats!" he hissed. "Who's afraid of the haunted castle? We're not! Come on you two. It's lunch-time! Tuck in!"

Max peeped out from his hiding-place at the gobbling ghouls. He thought there was something odd about those ghosts, especially the one that went 'dee-doo, dee-doo'!

He was just wondering what to do when he was stopped in his tracks.

A terrible howling came from above, and the blood froze in his veins. The Grabbly Gang looked up just in time to see two wailing white forms drift down from the castle battlements. Spine-chilling screeches filled their twisted black mouths.

"Eeeeeeeeeeee!" they hissed, and headed straight towards Gripper.

"Aaaargh! Help! Mummy!" The Grabbly boys were on their feet and running for their lives, taking shelter in the nearest place – the dungeons!

The two angry castle spooks turned their attention on the rest of the school. There was nothing odd about these ghosts. They were the real thing. They howled and hissed. They clawed the air with terrible talons and rushed down upon the children. There was no escape!

Chapter Five

The children scattered in every direction.
Even Miss Blossom had hidden herself
down the barrel of a big cannon. All you
could see were her feet sticking out at
one end.

Max thought fast. These ghosts were
on the rampage. What could he do? He
squinted at them through his father's
boggly spectacles, trying to get a clearer
view. Suddenly he pulled the glasses from
his nose and looked at them carefully.

He was wearing the Hypno-spex!
But would they work on spooky spooks?
There was only one way to find out. Max
switched them on, stepped out from his
hiding-place and stared straight at the
screaming ghosts. "Come and get me!"
he yelled.

The ghouls took one look at the twirling lenses, shuddered to a halt and hung in mid-air. Instead of screaming they just said, "Durrrrrrrrrrrr...?"

"Go and find those other ghosts and bring them back here," shouted Max.

Away went the spooks, while the children crept out from their hiding-places and pulled Miss Blossom out of the cannon.

"Oh Max, well done!" she cried. "What wonderful spectacles!"

A few moments later the Grabbly Gang came rushing out of the dungeon, screaming beneath their sheets, with the castle spooks in hot pursuit.

"Now let's see what sort of ghosts we have here," smiled Max, and he pulled away the bedsheets. "Well, well, well!"

"It's the Grabbly boys!" cried Miss Blossom. "How could you do this to us?"

But the Grabbly Gang could not say a word. Their teeth were chattering so much from fear that the only sound they made was, "Ddddddddddddddddddd."

Needless to say everything was sorted out nicely. The castle guides explained that they knew all about the castle ghosts. Normally they only came out at night when nobody was around. The Grabbly Gang had obviously upset them so much that they decided to spook the visitors. Max gave the guides the Hypno-spex, just in case there was trouble in the future.

The Grabbly Gang went home in disgrace and still shaking from their encounter. Max and his friends sat down and had their lunch in peace, at last.

When Max arrived home he told his parents about the ghosts. Max's dad was delighted. "I knew those spectacles would be useful," he grinned. "And now I shall show you my latest invention."

"It won't make horrible messes again, will it?" asked Max's mum.

"No, no, no. Take a look." Max's dad took the packet of Spooky Chunks and tipped it upside down. Nothing happened. Nothing fell out and there was no mess. Max took the packet from his father and stared inside.

"You've glued them into the packet!"
Max exclaimed.

"Exactly. That way they can't spread all over the table and floor and make a horrible mess."

"But you can't eat them either!" Max pointed out.

"Ah," frowned Max's dad. "Why does there always have to be a problem? Oh well, back to the drawing board I suppose." Max's dad sighed and plodded back to his inventing shed.

"What a strange man your father is,"
murmured Mum. "Right then, I'm going
to ski down Mount Everest. See you later."

Ginger jumped on to Max's lap. He
looked at Max as if to say, "You're not
going to put Spooky Chunks in my ear
again, are you?" and settled down for a nap.

Max smiled as he stroked the cat. Some people might think he lived in a rather strange house, but at least life was never dull!

Look out for more titles in the Red Storybooks series:

Dinosaur Robbers by Jeremy Strong

Tyranosaurus and Triceratops may look real, but they're actually two robotic dinosaurs invented by Max's dad. However, Buster's and Binbag's beady eyes spy the dinosaurs and decide they'll come in handy for a spot of burglary…

Max and the Petnappers by Jeremy Strong

Max is alarmed to discover that his goldfish has been petnapped. But not as alarmed as when he meets Aunt Claribel – the very large, very loud and very famous opera singer. So famous that the petnappers, Belladonna Snitch and Gretel Grapple, decide she must be worth a lot more money than any pet. Luckily, Max is on their trail…

Aliens in School by Jeremy Strong

Max thinks this will be the worst school fancy dress party ever. His friends are going to die laughing when they see him in his Father Christmas outfit. But on the day, the school is invaded by aliens – Gobbs from the planet Gobble intent on gobbling up all their party food. Everyone watches horrified as the Gobbs dive into the jelly. Max must do something, but what?

Frankie Stein's Robot by Roy Apps

Frankie Stein seems like an ordinary sort of lad. But he isn't. He's an inventor – that is, until Aunt Griselda comes to stay. She doesn't like his inventions. She insists that he spends all his spare time tidying up. Worst of all, she gives him huge, slurpy kisses. It's time for Frankie to invent something really spectacular – something that will leave Aunt Griselda speachless.

You can buy all these books from your local bookseller, or they can be ordered direct from the publisher. For more information about Storybooks, write to: *The Sales Department, Macdonald Young Books, 61 Western Road, Hove, East Sussex BN3 1JD*